I'LL BE YOUR SOMEBODY Preview

Rosita had known this day would come sooner or later. While she didn't contact Ulrich per se, she did get updates about him from Bevin, who would get calls from Tim whenever he could. Everyone was safe as of the last update, which had been two weeks ago.

Yeah, so safe he'll be at my place at any moment!

He'd only been here once, after his breakup with Patrice. During New Year's no less. The girl didn't have a sense of timing worth a damn. Patrice had been on her way back to Seattle to visit her folks; and when she hadn't invited Ulrich to come along, well, that had been quite the death knell. Since Tim had encouraged Ulrich to come down to South Carolina to ring in the New Year with friends, they'd somehow ended up at Rosita's condo, which made sense because having a wild party at Bevin's parents' house was nigh impossible—especially with baby Kerry in tow. To be fair, however, the party hadn't started crazy; but when one was friends with

Courtney and Tamara, bedlam was only a tick-tock away.

Rosita and Ulrich hadn't slept together then, surprisingly, but they'd had one hell of a make out session. Ulrich, despite his inebriation, had had too much respect for Rosita to treat her as a trampoline woman. But when she'd come up to visit Bevin and Tim during the Martin Luther King holiday, all bets had been off.

And clothes.

And all the hard-ass Rosita-ness she wore like a badge of honor. He'd coaxed that right off her with tender kisses, delicate touches, and succulent moans of pleasure in her ear.

Six months and several hookups later, here they were.

Praise for Savannah J. Frierson

"The emotional connection between the hero and heroine was superb."

Book Riot on *Trolling Nights*

"Reading *Be Mine* was like sinking into spicy candyfloss . . . There is nothing I love more than books that are both erotic and achingly romantic, and this one ticked that box."

Talia Hibbert, author of *Act Your Age, Eve Brown*, on *Be Mine*

"I loved this beautifully written, sexy and moving novelette . . ."

Ruby Lang, author of *Open House*, on "Grounded for Christmas"

"It deserves all the stars and then some."

Romance Novels in Color on *Being Plumville*

I'll Be Your Somebody

Savannah J. Frierson

To being somebody's somebody.

Author's Note

Please note this novelette features scenes and comments that may be upsetting, such as discussions of miscarriage, descriptions of trauma, childbirth, inebriation, and war/military imagery. I hope I have portrayed these moments with the grace and care necessary, but if you feel these themes may be too much to navigate, please protect your space, energy, and health however you may need.

Be well.

Savannah J. Frierson

I'LL BE YOUR SOMEBODY

One Predawn

Rosita was slow to open her eyes, to face the reality that she was here—again—with a heavy, muscular, dark-bronzed arm draped over her bare, russet waist. She bit her lip so she wouldn't moan when the arm tightened around her, bringing her back against a hard body that shouldn't give as sweetly as she knew it could...as it had last night while she imitated una vaquera.

But he'd been such a willing bronco.

"Rosita chica..."

Her eyes narrowed and her lips thinned. She could remember when he'd started calling her that, right before the wedding of their best friends Tim and Bevin Capshaw. Her mother had kept calling her *chica*, as was her right; but *he* had to take it a step further, thinking he was so clever because it rhymed. And now it stuck. Even Robbie called her that, but her brother lived to get on her nerves, knowing she loved him too much to kill him.

Soft, moist lips touched her naked shoulder and she shivered. “Rosa.”

She sighed and relaxed into him automatically, cursing herself for the unconscious action. He was the only man able to get away with calling her that other than her father...and sometimes her brother. But he’d called her Rosa last night as he slid inside her paradise over and over again. She hadn’t smacked him for it, just clutched his shoulders and bit at the crook of his neck and clamped around his cock so he would never, ever leave her.

“Rosa...”

Eyes drifting shut, she became spineless, especially when he pressed her back against the bedding and rose above her, his black eyes boring into her soul so deeply she couldn’t mask it with sass and no-nonsense—even with her eyes closed. He cupped her cheeks and let his broad nose touch hers, her legs opening so she could cradle him close, so he could enter her again, which he did.

She gasped and her eyes flew open, especially when he remained unmoving inside her as his cock throbbed with his heartbeat that matched hers evenly.

His expression was so serious, so different than it usually was. He had jokes for days, but nothing about this was a laughing matter.

She'd started coming up to Virginia Beach from Charleston nearly once a month or so since the New Year under the guise of checking on The Grind Virginia Beach location and seeing her best friend. So what she found the time to see *him*, too, so he could blow her back out like no other could? But even she had to admit it was more than that. And, truly, always had been.

Unable to help herself, she touched her palm to his cheek, her heart fluttering as rapidly as his eyes did, her body exhaling just as fully as his did.

"What you do to me," he whispered, turning his head to kiss her palm. "Rosa."

She kissed him, letting her tongue dance with his as he began to move inside her. He wasn't the biggest or the thickest, but he was still the best lover she'd ever had. This man possessed something none of the others had, and she was too chicken to say what it was.

Even though they both knew.

He wrapped his arms around her waist and brought her flush against him, his solid strength turning her softness to fuzzy cotton. She wound her legs around his hips and he ground into her, not leaving her warmth, but savoring it.

He settled his face into her neck and she dug her nails into the back of his head. This embrace was hard, intense. Breath squeezed from her lungs as her skin absorbed his.

"What you do to me," he whispered again.

It wasn't a question. It was acceptance of an answer.

Rosita trembled, feeling her heart opening wide even as she tried valiantly to shut it again. Her very own Pandora's Box, except it was receiving, not releasing.

He paused again, buried to the hilt inside her, his fingers kneading the small of her back. Rosita felt tears sting her eyes and she nestled her face into the crook of his neck. This was different from all the other times, even though it had started the same. He'd come down from Virginia Beach to Charleston with the Capshaws to visit Bevin's parents for Easter weekend. But somehow, he'd ended up here, at *her* condo, where she'd torn off *his* clothes so she could get fucked good and proper. And for the first few hours or so, he'd obliged her, talking filthy, being none too gentle—rough and raw. But then he'd started nuzzling her, started calling her *Rosa*, her name falling from his lips like stardust, pixie dust. She'd done a fair impression of Wendy Moira Angela Darling, and she'd cursed it as she relished it.

He shifted, settling onto his butt, never letting her go. She straddled him, reminiscent of the very first position they'd tried six hours ago, except they were both sitting up now. He scooted to rest his back against the headboard, his face still in her neck, his goatee scratching the silken, sensitive skin there.

"Ride me," he demanded, and she shivered again.

Rosita began undulating her hips, not sliding off his length because his arms were too powerful around her, too secure, too wonderful. He started kissing along her neck, across her collarbone, up to the point of her chin. His hands moved from the small of her back to her breasts, cupping their heavy weight, thrumming her chocolaty nipples. He continued to nip her chin and tweak her breasts while she just rocked upon his erection. She felt his eyes on her again, and she looked everywhere but at him. He had her too open as it was; she needed to guard some secrets for herself.

"When are we gonna stop this?" he asked breathlessly, moving his hands from her chest to wrap his arms around her waist again.

"As soon as I come," she hissed, her face pinched as she glimpsed the release she desperately needed.

There was a deep, breathless chuckle. "And then what, you go back to Bevin's until you need my cock to scratch your pussy's itch?"

She snapped her eyes to him and glared. "¡Sucio!"

He quirked an eyebrow. "¿Es la verdad, no?"

She averted her gaze and bit her lip, her climax and her shame warring within her. *No*, she said in her head, admitted to herself for the first time. He was not just a cock to scratch her itch. He hadn't been for a long time. In fact, she'd purposely stayed away from him that first night at The Barrel.

Patrice had clocked him first and he'd seemed more than happy with being her choice. He'd grown to have real feelings for her, too, but Patrice's didn't match his in intensity. The pretty Korean woman's upbringing was too strong an influence compared to how "nice of a guy" he was. She could never bring him home, and what she felt for him wasn't strong enough for her to risk her parents' disapproval. Rosita had admittedly lost a little respect for him because of how he'd just let Patrice walk away, despite the fact he was among the most elite fighters in the country. Patrice Yi had been his prototype, he'd said. Then why had he let her go? So what if he could shoot a rifle on target or knock a guy out with one punch? He couldn't stand up to a woman who was maybe five-four and a buck-ten soaking wet. Rosita needed a strong man, a man who would fight for her, a man who would fight *her* should she start tripping like Patrice had.

Be careful what you wish for.

"¿No es verdad, Rosita, chica?" he asked quietly in her ear, not moving, his body primed and ready to go upon her command.

She looked directly into his eyes. "You know it's not."

He smiled slowly, exposing the tiny gap between his two upper-front teeth, her heart opening wider and feeling the warm breeze of affection overcome her. "Good girl," he congratulated, thrusting into her hard. "Very good girl."

Rosita's eyes rolled into the back of her head. His thrusts were measured and deep, as if he were laying claim to her, marking her. She wanted to pull out of his arms. She wanted to meld into him. She wanted everything and was scared that he offered it to her and then some. She wasn't ready for this. Booty calls she could handle. She handled them very well. But this upping of the ante was far, far out of her comfort zone.

"Kiss me, Rosa," he husked against her cheek even as his mouth crept to hers. "Kiss me..."

She did, softly, nothing but lips, and yet it triggered her most powerful climax thus far. She felt him freeze also, then explode inside her, making her shake more violently than an 8.0 earthquake.

There were most certainly *not* tears in her eyes or rolling down her cheeks, but those were his fingers gently wiping away the moisture that had suddenly appeared on her face.

"Mi hermosa chica Rosita," he whispered against her nose before kissing it.

She couldn't help but laugh at that, curling her arms around his neck and hugging him close to her heart. He chuckled as well and returned the embrace just as fiercely.

"You are," he said quietly.

She sniffled. "I know."

He chuckled again. "You're not lacking confidence."

"Should I?"

"No," he replied, kissing her shoulder. "You certainly keep a brother righteous."

Rosita caressed the back of his head, staying silent. They sat quietly for a while, him still inside her, not as hard as he had been, but definitely not soft. Her internal muscles massaged him, more calming than arousing, and she took in a breath full of their scent. For some reason her mind went back to the past, months ago, years ago, back when Bevin had been a Moore. She remembered a conversation they'd had, sometime after the night Tim had told Bevin he loved her. Rosita had confessed to her best friend she'd never made love with a man before. Sex, yes—fuck, yes. Love? That had always been elusive.

It didn't feel so elusive anymore.

"I should pull out," he said against her temple.

"You should," she agreed, gripping his cock tighter.

He moaned. "Rosita, chica."

"I like you just where you are," she murmured honestly, letting her lips drift along his temple.

He kissed her neck and rubbed her back. "I do as well."

He didn't pull out, slinking back down onto the bed and drawing the sheet over them. She fell into slumber—him inside her, around her—having one of her best sleeps in months.

Ooh, boy, she was seriously fucked.

One Morning

The readout was missing three letters: N, O, and T. As in, "NOT PREGNANT."

There was not a sound to be heard, a breath to be breathed, a pulse to be pulsed. Rosita and Bevin stared at each other, she on the commode and Bevin on the side of the tub. Her best friend's golden eyes dropped to Rosita's midsection.

"*Lawdhavmercy*," Bevin rasped.

Rosita dropped the stick as if it had shot up a thousand degrees in one second and scrambled off the toilet. She stared wide-eyed at it, her mind telling her she'd suddenly become illiterate, that she did not read what she just read.

"No sé leer en inglés."

The shocked expression on Bevin's midnight-hued face melted into one of amusement. "Yes, you can read English. Very well, in fact. Welcome to the club, Rosita."

Rosita glared at her, two seconds away from sticking out her tongue and cussing her out in fluent Spanish, when a knock on the door made them both jump.

"Damn! What?" Rosita snapped.

"Uh, are y'all okay in there?"

Rosita's nostrils flared in frustration while Bevin's flared for an entirely different reason. Rosita sucked her teeth and rolled her eyes. "Hussy."

Bevin glanced down at the stick, then raised an eyebrow at her friend. "Pot, kettle, innit?"

"Bevin?"

"We're fine, baby," Bevin called to her husband, taking a few squares of toilet paper to pick up the stick and throw it in the trash. "You want to use the bathroom?"

"Yeah."

"Where's my child?"

"With his godfather."

"Is my child still alive?"

"Bevin," came the sigh, and Bevin grinned, washing her hands.

"All right, my love, we're on our way out," she promised, cutting off the water and drying her hands on one of the towels. Bevin opened the door and giggled as Tim gathered her close and gave her a gentle kiss on the mouth.

Rosita pretended she didn't notice any of this as she washed her hands as well, her heart squeezing at the possibility that could be her one day. Her and—

"Rosita," Tim greeted, kissing her cheek.

"Hello, Tim," she said, turning off the water. "Potty's all yours."

"You're too good to me," he moaned, putting his hands on his hips and following the women out with his eyes. Rosita shut the door. She couldn't help grinning as Bevin leaned against the wall and fanned herself.

"Been almost two years and I still can't believe it!" Bevin whispered.

"Well, you better," Rosita mumbled. "I have a feeling we'll soon be in another bathroom with another stick reading another result like the one we just got!"

Bevin approached her and grasped her hands. "Go to a doctor, Rosa."

"I know."

"Tell him, Rosa."

She didn't say anything to that, just squeezed Bevin's hands and took a deep breath. The bathroom door opened and the tall, broad, blond man gave them an odd stare, well, more Bevin than Rosita. Bevin stood straighter and returned her husband's expression.

"What?" she asked.

Tim didn't respond right away, but then moved and kissed his wife's forehead. "I love you."

Rosita almost laughed at the way Bevin melted, tipping up her head so Tim could kiss her mouth.

"I love you too," Bevin promised. Tim pulled back, the largest cheesy grin on his face, and began whistling horrendously off-key as he went back to the living room. Rosita laughed.

"¡Tu esposo ésta loco!"

Bevin grinned and started after her husband. "And yet someone has to love his crazy ass. Might as well be me!"

Rosita let that thought sink in, marveling at how simple it was in its wisdom. She didn't enter the living space fully, however, her feet getting stuck at the threshold as she watched *him* play with her godson—their godson.

Their son?

"Why're you standin' there, Rosita? Kerry doesn't bite!" Tim teased. Rosita cracked a smile when Bevin scoffed.

"Clearly someone's not ever breastfed a body!"

"Bevin!" Tim whined, wincing.

She gave him a perplexed glance. "What?"

"Don't be mentioning your..." He nodded to Bevin's chest. "In mixed company!"

Rosita fell out laughing at the disbelieving look Bevin shot her. "You hear this 'Bama bozo?"

"I don't mind—"

"Ulrich!" Tim cried, and Rosita heard a smack, then a joyous giggle. "That's my *wife*!"

"And she's fine as hell!" Ulrich said. "You see your daddy abusing Uncle U? He's a bad, bad daddy!"

More giggling bubbled forth, and Rosita finally entered the living room. *He* was lying on his back, holding up a beaming Kerry who was reaching tiny, burnished-gold hands toward *his* broad nose. Rosita glanced at the wedded couple, Tim's head in Bevin's lap as she played with tendrils of his hair and spoke softly to him.

"Roro!"

Immediately, Rosita sat down and held out her arms. Kerry reached for her in return, aided by *him* as he settled the baby in her embrace.

"Hey," Ulrich whispered, kissing Rosita's cheek as he pulled back.

"Hey," she said just as softly, Kerry beaming at her as he clapped his pleasure.

Ulrich sat across from her and gazed while Rosita gave all her attention to the child in her arms. She wanted to fidget, something she *never* did for *any* man, but Ulrich Brown wasn't just *any* man.

"Look at him all comfortable," Ulrich said softly, reaching out to trace a finger along Kerry's chubby cheek. The baby had snuggled into Rosita's chest, sucking on his thumb. Rosita had started rocking without even realizing it. "I'm jealous."

Rosita cut a look at him. "Stop it."

"Can't help how I feel, Rosa," he said quietly, keeping his focus on the baby, but his words wrapped all the way around her like a thermal blanket. There was no way she could respond to that, not with this particular audience, so she kept her mouth shut.

"I'm saying!" Tim piped up. "When Kerry was first born, I had a hard time not being jealous of my own son!"

"Timothy!" Bevin chastised.

"Calling me by my full name?" Tim moaned and pulled Bevin's face down to his. "What I told you about foreplay when we have people over?"

Bevin groaned and pulled her head up, pretending she wasn't amused by her husband's antics. "You are a mess!"

"And yet you married him anyway," Ulrich teased. "Methinks the one who isn't right in the head is you."

"Nobody asked for your two rusty pennies!" Bevin said, sucking her teeth and rolling her neck.

Ulrich glanced at Rosita. "Taking lessons from my Cuban firecracker, are we?"

Rosita's lip curled. "I didn't know you and my mama were tight like that."

Tim and Bevin practically died laughing; and because baby Kerry refused to be left out of the revelry, he started giggling as well. Rosita grinned and winked at a sulking Ulrich even as she cuddled her godson closer.

"Thinks she's so clever," Ulrich groused.

"I *am* clever," Rosita insisted and beamed. "Don't hate!"

Ulrich's expression cleared and he arched an eyebrow. "Who said I did? I like you, Rosita."

"Humph."

"You know very well how much I like you."

Suddenly there was a loud, hacking cough, and both looked up to see Tim rubbing Bevin's back and speaking in low tones to her. Rosita narrowed her eyes, knowing Bevin wasn't really in distress. Sometimes the woman could be a subtle as a 2x4 to the face.

"Ma! Ma!" Kerry called. Ulrich took the baby from her and handed him to Bevin. Rosita stood and went into the kitchen, her body rippling as she sensed Ulrich following her. Once they were out of sight, Ulrich spun her around and pressed her against the wall, dropping his face into her shoulder.

"I miss your scent," he whispered.

Rosita prayed her moan wasn't audible; but upon his chuckle, she knew she'd been heard. Deciding not to fight it anymore, she let her arms come around him.

His mouth traveled up her neck and across her cheek to settle against hers.

"I miss you," he said just as quietly.

Rosita squeezed her eyes shut, horrified by the tears that made a surprise guest appearance. They hadn't seen each other since Easter weekend. It was Memorial Day weekend now. And though they spoke to each other on the phone nearly every night, it wasn't the same.

She shook her head and hugged him fully. This was the first proper greeting she'd given him all trip. When he'd first arrived at the Capshaw house, he'd just given her a quick kiss and hug—nothing like the welcome he'd wanted to give and nothing like the welcome she'd wanted to receive.

"You're shaking, baby," Ulrich murmured as he squeezed her. "What's wrong?"

Rosita shook her head. "Nada."

"Me dices mentiras, Rosita, chica," he chastised in her other native tongue. "Whatever we are or have been, liars are not one of them."

She pulled back to gaze at him. He gave her a small smile and Rosita palmed his face with both of her hands. If she was what the stick said, she held the father of her child's face. That rocked her, especially because she'd always made sure to be careful with her partners. She was like clockwork with her birth control, and never had any fun without a raincoat.

Until Ulrich.

Suddenly, the trepidation she'd felt not even an hour earlier was conspicuously absent. Looking into his eyes, she saw nothing but honor and integrity. Why in the world had she been running so hard for so long, only stopping because the passion and need would be on the brink of exploding inside her? He'd been biding his time, patient, letting her come to him. Never the other way around.

"What I do to you?" she asked quietly, needing the answer. She had to know, needed to know before telling him she was also about to, potentially, make him a father.

Never taking his eyes from hers, he plucked one of her hands from his cheek and kissed the knuckles of it. "Make me better."

And he made her accountable, vulnerable, all the things she didn't like feeling. She'd gotten caught up once. She'd promised herself to never get caught up again.

But she didn't want him to let her go.

"Rosa," he said quietly. "What's wrong?"

She abruptly pulled out of his arms and began to pace the kitchen, hugging herself. Should she tell him, even if there wasn't official medical confirmation, about their possible impending parenthood? She knew Bevin would want her to, but Rosita was unsure.

So deep in thought, Rosita jumped and almost broke the skin of the thumb she'd been gnawing on when she felt large, sturdy hands grasp her shoulders.

"You're scaring me, baby."

Rosita leaned against Ulrich, nay, snuggled into him, and sighed. "Lo siento."

"I can't help if I don't know what to do," he told her, moving his hands to wrap his arms around her trim waist.

"But I don't know what to do, either," Rosita whispered.

He kissed the space where her neck met her shoulder. "Is it bad?"

She shrugged. "Es posible que no sea bueno."

"Hmm, why don't you tell me so we can determine if it's bad or not?" he suggested, holding her tighter and letting his nose drift along her cheek. The fact he was being this open with his affection while knowing either Bevin or Tim could walk in here at any moment astounded her. While their friends knew they had a "friends-with-benefits" situation, Rosita didn't think Ulrich was holding her the way he'd hold a booty call.

She looked down at their hands on her belly, their fingers tangled together. Her slim, russet fingers were protected by his thick, bronzed ones, and she squeezed them.

"Ulrich..."

Twin chirping sounds prevented her from saying anything else. Rosita's heart cracked when she heard Bevin murmur "*No!*" sadly. Keeping one arm around her, Ulrich pulled the beeper from his belt buckle and checked it.

"Shit."

Rosita clutched at his fingers, pressing their hands closer to her abdomen, to the place where their potential baby rested.

"We're being called, Rosa."

Panic lanced through her. She wondered how the hell Bevin did this on the regular. What did she say? What *could* she say? She couldn't tell him about this possible pregnancy now, at the very least not when she wasn't sure herself. Why make him worry about a maybe? She'd tell him when he returned if there was something to tell.

And he would *return.*

She faced him and looked into his black eyes, placing her hands right above his heart. "Ten cuidado, chico."

He quirked his lips and nodded. "Sí, Rosita, chica."

A loud wail blared into the kitchen, and Tim's deep voice began rumbling. Rosita and Ulrich went back to the living area where they saw Tim cooing and bouncing a sobbing Kerry, his duffel bag by his feet. Bevin was standing off to the side and looking at the floor, her arms tight around her.

"Da! Da!" Kerry cried, rubbing his face against his father's neck.

Rosita saw Tim's jaw clench as he held his baby gently to him, his green eyes closed. "Daddy has to work, okay?"

"No!" Kerry refused, burrowing closer.

There was a loud sniffle and Bevin wiped her face before going to Tim. "Come on, Kerry, Papa's gotta go."

"DaDa!" Kerry cried again, shaking his head and kicking his legs in denial.

Tim opened up his arms and brought Bevin close to him, whispering unintelligibly to his wife as he held her and his son to his heart. Rosita felt Ulrich press against her, tangling their fingers together.

"I get jealous of him," Ulrich said quietly in her ear.

"Why?"

"He has someone to say goodbye to," Ulrich said, shrugging. "I shouldn't be, you know? Yeah, I call my parents, but for years, Tim didn't have anyone he could call. But I see him now with Bevin and his son, and I wish I had someone like that."

Rosita turned to him. He still gazed at the family having their moment, wistfulness emblazoned on his face. She stood directly in front of him and his black eyes moved to her.

"I can be that for you today," she offered. "Si tú quieres."

He said nothing for a long while, so long Rosita's cheeks burned and she started to retract her proposal, until his large, dark-bronzed hand smoothed over the inky curls of her head to cup her cheek.

"Pray for me?" he asked quietly.

"Sí, siempre," she responded, not even bothering to hide the tears in her eyes.

He smiled a little, touching his thumb to her cheek, and kissed her forehead. "Gracias, mi hermosa chica Rosita."

"Regrese a mi, Ulrich," she commanded on a whisper, clutching his shirt. "Por favor."

"I'll do my best," he replied sincerely, and Rosita knew that was the only vow he could keep. They hugged each other for a long moment before Ulrich pulled away to drop a chaste, yet meaningful kiss to her lips. He then moved to hug Bevin and his godson while Tim came to her. He grinned, his tall frame enveloping her, and she snuggled into his form.

"Take care of her," Tim said.

"Of course. You know me."

"Yeah, and I know her." Tim pulled back and gave her a serious look. "She won't tell me."

"Tell you what?"

His eyes shifted down the hall and back to her. "I know."

Rosita frowned. "You know *what*?"

Tim pursed her lips. "She's pregnant."

She sucked in a harsh breath and her eyes widened. "What?"

"I saw the stick, Rosita. Why won't she tell me? She thinks I can't handle it?"

"Tim—"

"If I didn't have to go right now I'd challenge her on it," Tim said with a slight huff. "I had to go off once without her telling me, and now I'm going again. She can't keep doing things like that."

Rosita licked her lips and tried to keep the anxiousness from her eyes. "She probably doesn't want to tell you until she's absolutely sure." Tim rolled his eyes and Rosita slapped him lightly on the chest. "Seriously! Those things aren't one hundred percent."

His irritation lessened. "But she'd tell me if she was, right?"

Rosita showed a little smile. "I think so. The last time, y'all were newlyweds. This time, you already have Kerry. Why not another?"

He smiled as well, kissing Rosita's cheek. "Thank you for being my friend."

It was things like this that let Rosita know just why this man held her best friend's heart. For all his strength and power, the gentleness and gratitude Tim could show displayed his humility and honor.

The same way Ulrich could.

"Come on, man, Uncle Sam is an impatient bastid!" Ulrich teased, injecting levity in a grave situation.

Everyone chuckled. Tim tweaked Rosita's chin playfully and winked as he backed away. He gave his wife and son one last lingering look, mouthing, "I love you," which Bevin returned. Kerry waved forlornly at his father and Tim blew him a kiss. Rosita put her hands on her abdomen, feeling the flutters of this poignant goodbye.

She met Ulrich's eyes and didn't break the contact until he closed the door behind Tim.

At that moment, she prayed her child had eyes like her daddy.

One Afternoon

"¡Rosita, chica, tú necesite que decirle a Ulrich que tú estás embarazada!"

She scowled at the cake she was pulling out the oven, muttering under her breath. Of all the times for her mother to come down to Charleston and bother a body! Didn't the woman understand she couldn't tell Ulrich anything because she didn't know where the hell he was? And even if she did, this wasn't something to tell over the phone or in an email—especially when the relationship was undefined! Ulrich wasn't her husband—he wasn't even her boyfriend! The most she could do was take care of herself and the baby she carried until Ulrich returned.

And he *would*. He promised he'd do his best.

"Rosita!"

"¡Sí, Mama, sí, yo sé!" Rosita insisted, putting the pan on a wire rack and pulling off the oven mitts. Her mother's sable hand closed around hers and Rosita let her head drop slightly. The older woman kissed her cheek and Rosita smiled.

"My baby's to be a mother," Milagros murmured in English, patting her daughter's hand. "¡Que bueno!"

"Even though I'm not married?" Rosita asked quietly.

Milagros moved her hand to smooth down her daughter's head. "Only a matter of time."

Rosita gave her mother a weird look. "No entiendo."

Milagros took her hand and led her to the kitchen table where they sat, the hands still joined on the tabletop. "You want to know why your father and I aren't disappointed."

"Yes."

"Well, there's no point in getting upset," Milagros said. "What's done is done. But your father and I weren't under any delusions, either. We both know you and Robbie are...em...*active*, we'll say. But I taught you well. Beverly and I taught you very well."

Rosita grinned. Her mother and Mama Bevie had given her a birds and bees discussion she'd never forget!

"And then after what happened before...this was different." Milagros shrugged and smiled slightly. "This *feels* different, mija."

Rosita nodded. "It is."

Milagros smiled. "Yo sé. Ulrich is a good and honorable man. Any friend of Tim's has to be, no?"

Rosita nodded. When she'd told her parents she was pregnant a few weeks ago, they hadn't even asked who the father was. They'd known, which had surprised the hell out of her.

"You always knew where the other was," her father Juan had said softly. "That's why we knew."

"What are you talking about?" Rosita had asked.

"Tim and Bevin's wedding," her mother had replied. "You always knew where the other was."

Rosita had tried to play it off, saying they were the maid of honor and the best man, but her parents weren't idiots and they hadn't raised their children to be idiots, either. But being an idiot wasn't necessarily the same as being a coward. For all of her "take-no-shit" attitude, Ulrich had scared the piss out of her. And unless she was on a toilet, Rosita liked her piss in her bladder where it belonged. But his black eyes...his sturdy body...his dark-honey skin...his...*goodness*. All that fine-ness was too much to handle even for *her*. She was used to men eating out her hand as if they were ducks and she held the bread crumbs.

But Ulrich didn't want crumbs, at least not in the long run.

And, turned out, she was the same type of woman.

Then again, how could she not be? She *was* Milagros Velez's daughter.

"This is why you should tell him, mija; not only because it's the right thing to do, but because it's the *only* thing to do. A man like that would want to know, ¿verdad?"

Rosita nodded.

"Yes, so," Milagros paused and stood, going back to where the cake was cooling. "He'll be here shortly—"

"What!"

Milagros beamed at her daughter. "I called him and told him to come. He should be here soon."

Rosita clenched her jaw, glad she hadn't been standing or else she'd be sprawled on the floor from shock. She wanted to cuss someone out, but she wasn't stupid enough to turn her ire onto her mother. She wondered how in the blue hell Milagros had gotten her hands on his number—

She was going to kill Robbie!

"I see the bloodshed in your eyes, mija. Don't kill your brother."

Damn. There was no way she could flout a direct order like that. She'd just have to maim him very well.

"Is that why we're baking a cake?" Rosita asked, setting aside her plan of vengeance for later.

"Sí," Milagros answered. "Tu novio tendrá mucha hambre."

Rosita snorted at that. As much as she wanted to correct her mother and declare Ulrich wasn't her boyfriend, considering her current state, the denial would be laughable. Besides, Ulrich would eat anything within sight regardless if he'd just had a five-course meal five minutes earlier.

"The cake will be cooled by then?"

Milagros shrugged. "No sé, pero habrá comida para comer."

Rosita leaned back in the seat, her hand settling on her abdomen. Already toned from her daily, yet modified capoeira routines, her stomach was even firmer now because of the life she carried within her. She forced herself to take deep breaths even as her heart rate increased. Maybe she should've called him, should've prepared him. She'd known this day would come sooner or later. While she didn't contact Ulrich per se, she did get updates about him from Bevin, who would get calls from Tim whenever he could. Everyone was safe as of the last update, which had been two weeks ago.

Yeah, so safe he'll be at my place at any moment!

He'd only been here once, after his breakup with Patrice. During New Year's no less. The girl didn't have a sense of timing worth a damn. Patrice had been on her way back to Seattle to visit her folks; and when she hadn't invited Ulrich to come along, well, that had been quite the death knell. Since Tim had encouraged Ulrich to come down to South Carolina to ring in the New

Year with friends, they'd somehow ended up at Rosita's condo, which made sense because having a wild party at Bevin's parents' house was nigh impossible—especially with baby Kerry in tow. To be fair, however, the party hadn't started crazy; but when one was friends with Courtney and Tamara, bedlam was only a tick-tock aw ay.

Rosita and Ulrich hadn't slept together then, surprisingly, but they'd had one hell of a make out session. Ulrich, despite his inebriation, had had too much respect for Rosita to treat her as a trampoline woman. But when she'd come up to visit Bevin and Tim during the Martin Luther King holiday, all bets had been off.

And clothes.

And all the hard-ass Rosita-ness she wore like a badge of honor. He'd coaxed that right off her with tender kisses, delicate touches, and succulent moans of pleasure in her ear.

Six months and several hookups later, here they were.

"Thinking about him, chica?"

Rosita sat up abruptly, her knee hitting underneath the table. She cursed under her breath while her mother merely smiled.

"You think you know everything," Rosita muttered, rubbing the smarting spot on her knee.

"Porque yo sé todo," Milagros said, her smile wideneing, "acerca de mis hijos."

¡Dios! Would Rosita be that kind of mother? Would she be able to tell her children's mood just by the inclines of their heads or the inflections of their voices? Granted, Milagros had had twenty-nine years to learn about her, but was the learning curve shallow or steep?

She wondered if Bevin could already do it with Kerry.

So deep in thought, she jumped at the chime that echoed through the condo, knocking her knee on the table again.

"Tu novio está aquí, chica," Milagros predicted.

Rosita gulped.

Milagros chuckled a little. "Go let him in, mija."

Rosita stood slowly, her knees quaking far more than she preferred, and she walked to the door. She looked through the peephole and sagged against the wall.

He was here.

Taking a deep breath and whispering a quick prayer a Dios, Rosita opened the door, her hand instinctively cradling the slight pooch of her abdomen. Ulrich sported a scar along his right cheek but other than that, looked just as handsome as he had the last time she'd seen him.

She closed her eyes, tears suddenly gathering in them. The weight of that thought had hit her without warning. She'd taken for granted his returns before, but not anymore. Not when she carried the life they'd created inside of her.

"Oh, Rosita, chica," he whispered and pulled her close. "Don't cry."

She sobbed instead, as if to spite him, wrapping her arms tightly around him. "Me alegro que tú regresaste a mi."

Ulrich walked them inside of her condo, closed the door, and then leaned back against it, never letting her out of his embrace. He whispered soothing nonsense, brushing his hand over her curly black hair and squeezing her gently every now and again. She curled into his hard body, wanting him to never let her go, scared at the emotions coming from her.

Eventually he lifted her in his arms, cradling her like a baby, and walked them to the couch. He settled her in his lap and rocked her, kissing her forehead and temple at various points. She didn't know how long they sat like that; but when she finally settled down, he brushed away her tears and smiled.

"You sure know how to greet a brotha!" he teased.

Rosita had to laugh, glad he reverted to humor. "I'm sorry."

"No! I don't mind," he promised. "Bevin was the same way when Tim came back the first time."

And just like Bevin's first time, Rosita was carrying her man's first child in her womb. She became woozy at that realization.

"You don't look so good," Ulrich murmured, placing the back of his hand against her forehead. "Are you sick?"

Rosita closed her eyes and shook her head, taking away his hand and clutching it in her lap. "I'm not sick."

His nose grazed her cheek. "Oh. So then you're pregnant."

Her eyes popped open. "Ulrich!"

He didn't back down. "Are you?" He settled his hand on her abdomen and a smile filled his face. "It's mine."

It wasn't a question, which was good for him, or else she would've socked him good in the eye. Rosita watched his large hand move over her belly as if he could feel the child beneath. It hadn't moved yet. According to the doctor, it was too soon. But she wouldn't be surprised if her baby decided to move for her daddy.

"I'd suspected," Ulrich admitted, his focus still on his hand.

"You did?"

"Yeah. Tim started ranting about Bevin not telling him she was pregnant, about a stick in the bathroom when we left his house that day. I didn't correct him, because correcting him would turn the focus on me, and I wasn't ready for it yet."

"Correct him?" Rosita asked. She could dissect that one first.

"Yeah," Ulrich said. "No way in the world Bevin would keep something like that from him. She would've told him if she was pregnant."

"But I didn't tell you."

He looked at her intently. "You aren't Bevin."

She winced and started to pull back, but Ulrich tightened his arms around her. "No, don't go anywhere. I didn't mean that as a dis. Our relationship isn't the same as theirs."

"No..."

"And part of me is glad you waited until now."

"Why?"

"Because I can hold you and hug you and make sure you're doing well. I would've been a mess in the field, knowing you were back here taking care of my baby and I couldn't be there for you," Ulrich confessed, his black eyes dancing over her features.

Rosita curled her hand around his. "Are you angry?"

He shook his head and kissed her. "I'm not even on the planet of Angry. I'm scared to death, though."

Rosita chuckled against his mouth. "I am too."

"You know I'll be here for you," Ulrich promised, letting strands of her hair curl around his fingers.

"I know. You're a good man."

"Yes. I..." He closed his mouth and laughed lightly. "You might snatch my head off."

"What?"

"I want to marry you."

The panic was swift and sure as it enveloped her body. She left his lap and stood, hands on her hips. "Because I'm pregnant?"

"It's certainly a factor."

At least he didn't lie to her. "And if I weren't pregnant?"

He shrugged. "I would've asked you eventually."

Rosita tilted her head to the side and stared at him. "Are you serious?"

He nodded, smiling slowly at her. "And for the record, you're the first woman I've asked to be my wife."

"Am I the first woman you've gotten pregnant?" Rosita said, going for the acerbic instead of the affectionate.

Ulrich frowned at her, then arched an eyebrow and leaned against the couch, cool as you please. "Yes."

Well, all the wind was knocked right out of her sails at that. She stumbled back and plopped down on the ottoman of the easy chair behind her, Ulrich shooting forward and holding out his arms to her.

"Careful! That's my baby you're carryin', woman!"

Rosita dropped her face so he couldn't see her automatic grin and she touched her stomach. Her grin then faded away as she realized what a hypocrite she was.

"This isn't the first time I've been pregnant, Ulrich."

She said it quietly so her mother wouldn't overhear although Milagros already knew about it. Rosita had closed her eyes, so she started when she suddenly felt hands on her thighs and the cool press of lips on her forehead.

"You miscarried," he guessed.

She met his eyes. "How—?"

"Besides the fact you were raised Catholic?" he asked, shrugging. "You would've found a way to raise that baby."

She nodded and let him hug her. She buried her face in his shoulder, taking the comfort he offered her. She *would've* found a way to raise her child, even after its punk-ass father left, screaming it wasn't his despite the fact *he'd* been the one to take her virginity and *he'd* been the only dick she'd ever fucked up until that point.

Her mother was right. This *was* different. Ulrich had claimed the baby immediately, as if the very thought it could be someone else's child never entered his mind, even though they weren't exclusive or even a couple. He'd offered to marry her, although as much as her heart fluttered at the prospect, she wouldn't hold him to it.

"Ulrich! Hola, chico, how are you?"

Milagros came out of the kitchen and placed the cooled and now frosted cake on the coffee table. Ulrich stood and hugged Milagros warmly.

"Hola, Mrs. Velez," he said, kissing her cheek as they broke apart. "How are you?"

"Bien," she murmured. Milagros's eyes sparkled as she looked between Ulrich and Rosita. "Did she tell you?"

Ulrich nodded and hunkered down in front of Rosita once more. "She did. I'm glad she did."

"And how do you feel?" Milagros asked.

"Jittery," Ulrich said, taking Rosita's hands in his.

Milagros smiled widely. "¡Muy bien! ¡Él será un buen esposo para ti, chica!"

Smirking slightly, Ulrich brought the backs of Rosita's hands to his lips. "Estoy de acuerdo."

She sniffed and looked away from her mother and her child's father, unwilling to give them the satisfaction of letting them know she thought he'd make a good husband as well.

One Dusk

The Capshaw household was still full of lovely smells that made her stomach turn. They'd just finished Thanksgiving dinner. The women were inside the kitchen and having a great time gossiping while the men were watching a football game that had them shouting and cussing every four seconds.

Rosita was in Kerry's room holding the eighteen-month-old to her heart as he slept. She'd offered to change the toddler while Bevin and the others cleared the table, but the little boy had beguiled her so sweetly with his smile as she did so that she'd started cooing and playing with him, enjoying his innocent laughter. She'd begun singing a Cuban lullaby her mother had sung to her, and Kerry had drifted to sleep. She probably should've put him in his crib, but she was too comfortable, and he was too heavy for her to stand without assistance, especially since she was now in her third trimester. Her center of gravity was all out of whack, and she became winded taking more than five steps, it seemed.

Kerry nuzzled his cheek against her collarbone briefly before settling back down. Rosita smiled and closed her eyes, rubbing his back with gentle circles as she allowed this brief peace to infuse her soul.

"Hey."

Rosita opened her eyes and swallowed as the woman, only a shade lighter than her own mother but maybe fifty pounds heavier, entered the room. Her relaxed hair was pulled back with a headband and her "granny" glasses looked stylish on her square face. She sat in the other rocking chair in the room, staring at the baby with a small smile.

"Practicing?" she asked.

Rosita nodded. "Yes, ma'am."

The woman frowned and waved away the greeting. "Oh, child, don't call me that. Call me Evelyn. Or Mom."

Rosita smiled patiently. "Miss Evelyn."

Evelyn gave a slight pout. "You'll call me Mom eventually."

Rosita merely nodded, not giving the woman any more ammunition than she already had.

Evelyn reached out and smoothed a hand over Kerry's soft head. "He's a beautiful baby."

"He is. He looks like both his parents."

Evelyn smiled. "I hope your baby looks like you."

Rosita laughed softly, careful not to wake up Kerry. "Your son isn't all that bad to look at!"

Evelyn chuckled as well. "I know that. He's a gorgeous man, my son!" She shook her head and sighed. "What I mean, is I hope you have a daughter."

Rosita grinned. It seemed all the women in her life wanted her to have a little girl. She'd expressly asked the obstetrician not to tell her the sex of the baby. She wanted it to be a surprise. Ulrich, however, was getting antsier by the second, but he'd just have to live like that for a few more months.

"Rosita, why aren't you and Ulrich married?"

Rosita shrugged and shook her head, unwilling to go there with Ulrich's mother. Hell, she hadn't even told *her* mother why—she hadn't even told *Bevin*. She could only handle a few things on her plate at a time; and right now, this baby she carried took up the whole plate.

There was also a matter that maybe Ulrich hadn't confessed to Miss Evelyn.

"He hasn't asked me."

Evelyn's eyes widened in surprise. "He hasn't?"

"No, ma'am. He's said he wants to, but he's never asked."

Evelyn nodded slowly and stood. "Oh, well, then, that just changes the entire story, don't it?"

Rosita raised her eyebrows. "Ma'am?"

"Humph," Evelyn said, wagging her finger at Rosita. "Changes the entire story, indeed!"

"He left out some key details, didn't he?" Rosita asked knowingly.

"My child." Evelyn huffed. "If I didn't love him so much—"

"You'd strangle him," Rosita finished.

Evelyn grinned. "Oh, you're already thinking like a Mommy."

Rosita laughed. "Have you *met* Milagros Velez?"

"I love her! She's teaching me to cuss out Alvin in Spanish!"

"And I'll bet my dad is teaching Mr. Alvin how to sweet talk you in Spanish too."

A glazed look entered Evelyn's eyes. "I can't wait!"

Laughing and throwing a wink at her, Evelyn left the room. Rosita shook her head with amusement, gazing down at Kerry once more. She wondered if that was what she had to look forward to in a marriage with Ulrich: gentle teasing, a healthy amount of lust, unfailing adoration, mutual and genuine respect. Rosita had to admit she was lucky. Just about all of the married couples in her life had all of those things. She could admit she'd taken it for granted, and had even thought it wasn't for her after that one horrendous relationship that resulted in her first, and thus far only, miscarriage. But it actually wasn't until seeing Bevin with Tim did it really hit home for her—men of their fathers' generation weren't extinct. They existed, and if one were patient and a little particular, one could find such a man for herself. Bevin had, though she'd done the exact opposite of what all those women's magazines said women should do to snag a man: be a single-digit size; flirt; pretend for the first x-months. Whatever. Bevin had been herself—insecurities, inexperience, and all—and Tim had basically told her, "I don't care, I love you anyway." Rosita couldn't help but get a little hope from that, even if, in the back of her mind, she'd never expected it to bear fruit.

But boy, did it ever! she thought to herself, smoothing a hand along her distended tummy. She chuckled, and then her smile widened when she heard an answering one.

Looking down, she saw her godson grinning at her. She let her nose touch his, and he giggled even more.

"I love you," she whispered, her heart suddenly becoming full of the emotion.

"Roro!" Kerry replied, turning his face to the space where her heart beat. Rosita held him closer, wondering if she felt this buoyant holding someone else child, would she float right out her seat while holding hers.

"I can already tell motherhood will suit you just fine. Not that I had any doubt."

Rosita didn't bother opening her eyes. "I'm stealing your son."

"Good luck. Tim knows where you live!"

Snickering, Rosita opened her eyes and stuck her tongue out at Bevin, who merely gave a smile reminiscent of her child's. She glowed, her midnight skin seeming to shine as if a full moon rose within her, and Rosita gasped.

"Are you pregnant *again*!"

Bevin, despite her dark hue, blushed and ducked her head, touching her middle. "Tim seems to think so. I haven't taken the test yet."

Rosita rolled her eyes and huffed. "Tim would keep you perpetually knocked up if he could!"

Bevin laughed at that. "Well, he needs to have another plan. So easy for him to make decisions when he doesn't have to carry them out!"

Rosita arched an eyebrow. "You know good and well you don't mind."

Bevin rolled her eyes but smiled a little. "Not *too* much. I certainly love the end product," she whispered, staring at her baby. She then looked at Rosita with contrition. "I don't mean to steal your thunder if I am."

"What do you mean?"

"This is your moment," Bevin insisted, her eyes dropping to Rosita's tummy. "And here come me and my horny husband rainin' on your parade—"

"Misery loves company," Rosita said dryly.

Bevin laughed, which caused Kerry to squeal and turn his head to his mother. Bevin clapped and approached them, relieving Rosita of her bundle as mother made silly faces at her son. Not five seconds later, the door opened revealing Tim and Ulrich, the former heading directly for his family while the latter came straight to her.

Ulrich glared mildly at Rosita, putting his hands on his hips. "You got me in trouble!"

"Shouldn'ta lied to your mama like that!" Rosita said unapologetically, putting her hands primly on her belly.

"Ha!" Tim exclaimed, sitting in the free rocking chair and bringing his wife and son onto his lap. Kerry reached immediately for his father's nose, which Tim shook out of the way, making Kerry squeal further.

Ulrich's glare intensified as he stared at his best friend. "Did anyone ask *you*?"

"Nope, but my house, I can share my opinions freely," Tim announced.

"And you let him get away with this?" Ulrich asked Bevin.

She shrugged. "I mean, he can give 'em, don't mean I have to take 'em!"

"Ha-ha! That's my woman!" Ulrich cheered, going to Bevin to give her a high-five. Tim glowered at them both.

"I don't get no respect!" Tim said in a very good imitation of Rodney Dangerfield.

"That's because it's earned, baby," Bevin chastised, even as she placed a kiss upon his pouting lips. When they broke apart, Kerry finally succeeded in grabbing his father's nose, and Tim rolled his eyes exasperatedly. "What did I say!"

Chuckling, Ulrich and Rosita looked at each other. He bent down on his haunches and placed his hands on her belly. "How are we doing?"

Rosita playfully palmed his head. "We are fine."

Grinning, Ulrich kissed her tummy and she kissed the top of his head. "Good to hear."

"I think so too," she said cheekily.

Looking very pleased with himself, Ulrich sat fully on the floor and leaned his head against Rosita's abdomen. The baby inside her pressed against the uterine wall as if in greeting and Ulrich kissed her belly again.

"I can't wait to meet you," he murmured, circling her protruding belly button.

"Stop that," Rosita whispered hoarsely, blinking rapidly at the sudden moisture that filled her eyes.

"Stop what?" Ulrich asked, a corner of his mouth rising in soft amusement.

Rosita sniffed and touched her cheeks, pointedly ignoring the attention Bevin and Tim were giving them. "You know what."

Ulrich stood on his knees once more, his face right in hers as his hands framed her pregnant bulge. "I'll stop when you give me what I want."

Rosita sniffed again, trying for a haughtiness she certainly didn't feel. "Greedy—"

"Why are you fighting me?" he asked, bringing his face closer so their noses touched. "Your parents love me, I love them; my parents love you, *I* love you."

It was the first time he'd said it, and the fact he'd said it with witnesses present made it impossible for Rosita to dismiss the claim. Words and tears clogged her throat. She couldn't do anything but shake her head.

"Tú eres una buena mujer y serás una buena madre, la madre de mis hijos. Estoy muy alegre que tú serás la madre de mis hijos, chica, muy alegre," Ulrich whispered against her mouth.

Rosita knew he'd asked someone, probably her father, how to say that in Spanish, because while Ulrich knew enough to be conversational, that speech sounded too practiced to be off the cuff. Nevertheless, she was still touched by the effort, that he wanted her to know in her co-native tongue how he felt about their upcoming parenthood. She wasn't just some chick he'd happened to knock up and would now do right by, he was truly glad.

"Oh, baby," she managed to squeeze out her throat, cupping the back of his head with both of her hands.

"Cásate conmigo, por favor," he continued, his voice trembling with the request. "Marry me."

She let her forehead settle against his and allowed the tears to flow freely down her cheeks. Ulrich rubbed her abdomen, as if their child could give him the strength to withstand any answer she gave.

"What if I say no?" Rosita asked.

"Then I will just ask again," Ulrich promised. "Just so you know, nobody else is being a father to my child but me as long as I'm alive, you understand?"

Well, damn! Rosita had to laugh a little. "I'm not an easy woman, Ulrich."

"No quiero algo fácil, chica. Te quiero a ti," he insisted.

"Lawd, Jesus, tell the man yes!"

Both Ulrich and Rosita turned to see a sobbing Bevin glaring at them, Tim grinning as he calmed down his wife with gentle words whispered against her temple. Kerry, perfectly comfortable against his mother's chest, raised a golden hand and nodded. "Roro!"

Nuzzling her tears away with his cheek, Ulrich whispered in her ear. "Even our godson approves, Rosa."

It certainly seemed that way. "When would this happen?"

"Hell, we could get married Saturday. There's no waiting period in Virginia."

"That soon?" Rosita asked.

"The sooner the better," Ulrich said, standing and helping her to her feet also. He wrapped his arms around her and she settled her cheek against his shoulder. "As outdated as the thought may be, I would like for you to be my wife when you birth my child, not just my baby's mama."

"We still have months to go—"

"We might get shipped out," Ulrich reminded her quietly in her ear.

Rosita tightened her arms around him and looked at Bevin and Tim. She spoke silently to her best friend, who nodded her dark head and settled further into her husband's embrace.

It's so worth it.

To be honest, Rosita had never wanted a huge wedding, and all the really important people were here. Tamara and Courtney would understand; hell, they'd been gnats in her ear asking her why she and Ulrich hadn't made it official yet. Even Patrice had seemed supportive, although their relationship was strained because of their obvious common denominator being Ulrich. But Patrice was happy with her new man, at least seemed to be, helped by the fact her parents were happy with him as well.

Patrice made her decision.

It was time for Rosita to make one as well.

"Your heart is safe with me," she ensured him, her mouth next to his ear.

Ulrich chuckled, bringing her closer. "That's good. What about my hand?"

"Your hand?"

"Yeah, baby, will that be safe with you too? Will you let me have yours in return?"

She didn't answer immediately, taking his hands and settling them on her belly before covering them with hers.

Rosita looked into Ulrich's glorious black eyes and smiled.

"Yes."

One Evening

She hadn't been this nervous…ever. Not even her first time having sex had filled her with such knee-freezing trepidation. She closed her eyes as she felt Ulrich move behind her, unable to stop her body from quaking when his soft, full lips touched the curve of her bare shoulder while he pulled down the zipper of her strapless, ecru organza dress.

"Tú eres tan hermosa, chica," he whispered against her trembling russet skin. "You make me breathless."

That feeling was certainly mutual, and she sagged against him, his tender hands moving along the front of her gaping gown, kneading her tummy. Their child was still, as if knowing they needed a moment to themselves.

A moment to consummate their wedded union.

Rosita raised her arms behind her and wound them around his neck as he moved his mouth up the column of her throat to her jaw. His hands pushed down the wealth of fabric covering her body, revealing her silk strapless bra and her silk bikini panties. She watched his bronze hands drift over the copper brown of her abdomen, the gold of his ring on his left hand glinting faintly in the room. His tongue snaked out to tease her pulse point and her breath caught.

"Ulrich."

"Yes, Mrs. Brown?"

Rosita's eyes rolled into the back of her head, her nipples growing tighter at the use of her new title. *Mrs. Brown.* She never knew being called a *Mrs.* Somebody would sound so erotic.

His hands left her stomach to unhook her bra. Ulrich moaned, cupping her breasts gently in his hands.

"So fucking beautiful," he whispered in her ear, right before kissing her cheek.

Rosita didn't care he was still fully dressed and she was only in her panties and thigh-highs, she'd never felt so beautiful in her entire life, and her earlier anxiousness melted into full-out arousal.

"Look at what I did to you," Ulrich muttered, bending his head over her shoulder so he could glimpse her swell. "Look at what I did, Rosa."

She turned her head and kissed the hair of the goatee lining his jaw. "Look at what you did, Daddy."

Groaning, Ulrich met her lips with his, his fingers sliding beneath the elastic of her panties, over the mons of her vagina, to her well-saturated slit. His thick fingers thrummed her clit, and Rosita rocked against the rhythm he set.

"So wet for me," he whispered against her mouth.

"Tan mojada por ti," Rosita agreed.

He nipped her upper lip as he let his finger slip inside her. She clamped around the digit and both of them hissed.

"Esta es mia," he mumbled against her cheek.

"Sí, es tuya."

His fingers lingered for another moment, then he removed them from between her legs, making her mew in protest. He kissed her shoulder again before standing in front of her, his eyes hooded and heady with a heat that set her ablaze. This was much different from how he'd looked at her earlier, during their small wedding with just them, the Capshaws, and the marriage commissioner at the courthouse. Barely a week had passed between the proposal and the wedding, chiefly because she was far advanced in her pregnancy and Ulrich didn't know when Uncle Sam would call.

"You need to be my wife the next time he does," he'd told her, and she'd agreed. They didn't have the luxury of idyllic. Her fault, but she'd already forgiven herself for it.

She managed to find a wedding dress to rent from a local maternity store and he wore a standard suit. The grand ceremony with all the family and friends at Founders Inn or some other swanky hotel would happen later. Maybe a year from now when the baby could at least babble and crawl.

For now, they'd have to settle for a wedding night at the swanky hotel, instead.

But those were considerations for a different time because that reverential look entered his eyes again, the same look that had been there when he'd recited his vows to her, as Ulrich sank to his knees. Never breaking his gaze, he rolled down the thigh-high stockings she wore, kissing her knees, then her thighs, once they were bared. He buried his face into her abdomen and kissed her tummy, and the baby pushed back in reply.

"I'm going to love your mother, now," he whispered against Rosita's belly button. "Hope we don't disturb you too badly!"

Rosita laughed, raking her nails gently along his head, the short hairs of his head feeling good against her fingertips. Ulrich groaned and leaned back, his eyes rolling in their sockets with pleasure.

"What you do to me," he murmured.

Rosita smiled. "Love you."

He grinned. "Damn straight you do."

Ulrich eased her into a sitting position on the bed, then stripped out of his suit. Her mouth went dry as her eyes drank in every muscular curve of his toned body. Her lips tingled with the urge to kiss and suck the light-caramel hue of his skin, and she slid her hand over her belly back between her legs.

"Fuck, Rosa," he muttered.

She grinned and spread her legs wider, making sure he could see her slim fingers dancing along her drenched passage.

"You are so damn beautiful," Rosita said to him. "Mi esposo es tan guapo, viril, y masculino."

Ulrich licked his lips and shucked out of his pants and underwear, leaving him fantastically nude to her greedy gaze. The long, hard, thick length of him jutted from the patch of inky curly hair below his stomach, and his hands closed around it, stroking. Her pussy clenched around her fingers in anticipation, wanting that inside instead of its paltry substitution. Her left hand dug into her thigh, the half-carat diamond of her platinum engagement ring, settled atop her platinum wedding band, twinkling in the muted light of the suite.

He came closer, though he didn't stop stroking himself. When he kneeled before her, her fingers stopped moving, frozen at the prospect of his next action.

"Spread your legs," he ordered.

Rosita almost came right then and there. She had magnificent memories of his mouth on her. Sometimes she'd be too tired for intercourse because he'd ring out multiple orgasms from her. But Ulrich was an unselfish lover, allowing her to lie there in bliss as he stroked her to yet another ecstatic plane with his cock deep within her.

Once she was wantonly displayed before him, Ulrich buried his nose into her pussy, the tip of it becoming saturated with her feminine dew. Rosita collapsed fully upon the bed as one of his hands kneaded the interior muscles of one of her thighs.

"You smell good," he groaned, his cheek against the lips of her vagina. "Jesus, thank you."

She arched herself into his face, the beginnings of her release gripping her body at the first long, lazy lick of his rough tongue. His other hand came up and splayed her wide, the cooler air of the room competing with the warmth of his breath. He kissed her gently and her clit swelled.

Ulrich chuckled. "Damn, girl! I love watching you grow."

"Ulrich, please!" Rosita whispered frantically. She was too close for him to play around.

His tongue teased her nubbin and she arched off the bed. His thumbs played with her labia before his teeth joined the fray.

"Better than the wedding cobler," Ulrich declared, licking his lips obscenely.

Rosita didn't know whether to laugh or scream at him to get her off; but when he sucked her pussy with the suction of a vacuum, she shouted in a language not even she knew.

"Yeah, baby," he said with complete cockiness. "I like it when I make you scream in tongues."

She writhed against his mouth, her orgasm whipping her to and fro on the bed. Rosita barely registered him creeping up her body, bestowing gentle kisses to the baby she carried, or taking quick sucks from her nipples, before he was suddenly above her. His lips melded to hers, the head of his cock brushing against her center.

"Look at me, Rosa," he said upon pulling back.

She did immediately.

"Watch your husband make love to you."

Rosita came again, and he wasn't even good and inside her yet. Undeterred, Ulrich thrust into her hard, making her gasp as her internal muscles fluttered around his dick.

He dropped forward, stopping himself just in time so he didn't crush her or his baby beneath his weight. Rosita wanted to wrap her legs around his hips like she used to, but there was a belly in the way and he was pumping too fast for her to gain any real purchase.

Ulrich settled his face into her chest, kissing her heart over and over again before rubbing his cheeks against her breasts.

"*So fucking beautiful*," he growled into her sweat-slicked skin.

Rosita couldn't really do anything but lie there, he was loving her so well. She had enough strength to let her hands glide over the muscles of his back to the small of it, but then he reared up so he could thrust deeper, harder, more profoundly.

His hands palmed her breasts, squeezing so her nipples ground into their centers, and Rosita felt herself leak even more. When he bent his head to suckle her, Rosita held his head to her chest and sat up enough to kiss the top of his head.

"Te amo, mi esposo," she whispered, feeling a little ball inside her expand to supernova size. "Te adoro mucho."

Ulrich kissed her above her heart once more, then at the center of her collarbone, the center of her throat, the underside of her jaw, the center of her chin, her mouth. He remained there, sucking her breath inside his body. Rosita framed his face to keep him from moving, and that little ball had suddenly become a giant one, exploding inside of her so she exclaimed her joy into his mouth. Seconds later, she felt the warm jets of his climax coat her insides, and Ulrich gathered his arms underneath her and gentled the force of his mouth upon hers.

"Damn, Mrs. Brown," Ulrich gasped, nipping the point of her chin. "Damn."

Rosita smiled, letting her fingers trail over the bridge of his nose to his mouth. "Yes, Mr. Brown?"

Ulrich's tongue struck out to twirl around her finger, sucking on it for a moment before letting it drop out with a pop. "Holding everything back until now, eh?"

"Didn't think you could handle it before," she said saucily.

He chuckled, moving down her body to cradle her belly. "I hope you're all right in there. Your Mommy tends to get Daddy real excited, so he has to return the favor."

Rosita giggled, drifting her hands along his head as Ulrich continued talking to their unborn child. She listened to the promises he made, promises Rosita knew he'd do everything in his power to keep because he was a man of honor.

And because he was a man of honor, Uncle Sam needed him.

Now.

Neither said anything or moved anything as that damnable chirp echoed through the room. Ulrich let it go for a full minute before leaving the bed to check his pager.

Rosita sat up, leaning against the headboard, amazed at the masculine beauty he possessed. Even nude with his penis semi-flaccid and a frown marring his face, Rosita thought he'd been fashioned by Dios himself, so exquisite he was to her.

Rosita saw his jaw clench, as well as his hand around the tiny machine, then he tossed the beeper onto the easy chair in the room and stood with his hands on his hips.

"Fuck."

Rosita closed her eyes and took a deep breath. She'd be strong. She'd known when she'd started this relationship he could be called at any moment. She'd just never thought it'd be *this* moment, during their wedding night.

She felt him come closer, crawling over her body as he gently lowered his atop hers. He kissed her softly.

"I have to go," he told her.

"I know," Rosita said.

"Open those beautiful brown eyes, Rosita, chica."

She did, smiling at his smile. He glided the backs of his fingers along her cheek and smiled wider.

"What?" Rosita asked, wondering why he grinned like that. Despite her smile, she found nothing about this situation that was pleasant.

"Thank you."

"For the nookie before you go off?"

He glared at her and tweaked her nose. “None of that, Rosa, not right now.”

He couldn’t tell her what to do. He couldn’t tell her not to be pissed off or spoiled or scared to motherfuckin’ death about his safety.

He couldn’t tell her not to be sad.

“Rosa,” he said again, cupping her cheek, the ring on his hand cool to the touch.

“What?” she repeated, but with less bite than before.

He grinned again. “Thank you for being my somebody.”

Shit. She’d intended not to cry, but then he had to say something sweet like that. He brushed her tears away with his cheek and lips, his hands rubbing her belly soothingly.

“I’ll always be your somebody,” Rosita vowed. “Soon, you’ll have two, and I promise to give you as many more somebodies as you’d like.”

He beamed at her, then moved his mouth to her belly button. “You’re a witness, lil’ one, so when your mother starts trippin’ when she’s carrying your little brothers and sisters, I want you to remember this conversation!”

Rosita slapped his shoulder lightly at that.

Still chuckling, Ulrich kissed all over her bare stomach, murmuring “I love you, I love you,” after each buss. Rosita didn’t bother to not cry anymore, letting her husband sip the tears from her cheeks before kissing her lips once more.

"Te adoro, mi esposa," he whispered against her mouth.

"I love you, too, Ulrich."

He left the bed and dressed quickly. Rosita put on his wedding dress shirt and helped him pack, stealing one of his T-shirts for later use. He grinned at her.

"You tell youngin' not to come before I get back," Ulrich said to her, zipping up his bag after making sure he had everything.

"I will."

He snorted. "And I bet she'll take after you and be ornery, come all early."

Rosita grinned. "And you'll continue to love her. Or him."

Ulrich kissed her forehead. "You're giving me a daughter. I can feel it."

They walked to the door, his rolling suitcase gripped hard in his hand. Rosita leaned against him, breathing in his scent. Ulrich rested his forehead against the top of her head.

"Regrese a mi, mi esposo," she whispered, her hand above his heart. "Regrese a nosotros."

"I'll do my very best," Ulrich vowed. She pulled back so he could kiss her mouth sweetly, and with a final graze of his hand against her tummy, he went down the hall. Rosita watched him until he turned the corner, out of sight, but never out of her mind or heart.

One Midnight

"I'm going to kill him."

The fact it was a calm statement and not a frantic exclamation struck fear in those who heard her. Rosita didn't care. All she cared about was the fact their child had held up its end of the bargain for as long as it could, but Ulrich still wasn't here. Hell, the baby had even held on for a few extra days after the doctor's projected due date. But still, Daddy Ulrich made no appearance. Nevertheless, the baby wanted out, and it was taking a battering ram to Rosita's birth canal to accomplish it.

"*Aaarrrggghhh!!*"

"You're doing great," Bevin assured her, taking a damp towel to Rosita's forehead to mop up the perspiration there.

Rosita rolled her eyes and tried to take deep, relaxing breaths. But the little terror inside her was making that nigh impossible.

"Get it out."

"Rosa—"

"I want this *fucking* thing out me *now*! Fuck, Ulrich! Why the fuck isn't he here?!" She heard Bevin murmur excuses for her friend's potty mouth.

"Shoot, I doubt she'll be the worst we have today!" one nurse cracked.

Rosita smiled with vindication—right before releasing another string of filth as the next contraction attacked.

She sagged heavily against the bedding once it passed and Bevin tsked behind the mask she wore, feeding her ice chips. "Seeing you like this makes me wonder why the hell I let myself get pregnant again."

Rosita smirked, eyeing her friend's slightly distended belly beneath the puke-green scrubs she wore. "Because you're a horny bitch for that fine-ass hubby of yours."

Bevin's golden eyes shone. "You right."

Rosita laughed a little, then she grasped Bevin's hand. "They'll be back, won't they?"

Bevin nodded. "They better be, or we'll be very put out."

Rosita nodded as well, dropping her friend's hand in favor of the guardrails as she went through another contraction. She'd been at this for hours; she'd long stopped counting after the fourth one. Aunt Bevie and her mother were watching Kerry in the lobby, there just in case Ulrich somehow managed to receive the message his wife was in labor.

"Damn, just somebody cut the fucker out!" Rosita growled.

"We'll give it a few more hours before it comes to that," her obstetrician said. Rosita merely glared, grinding on the molars of her teeth.

She knew her body, however, and it didn't have a "few more hours" before it fell apart. Rosita felt as if she were being split into halves, and *where were her gotdamn drugs*!

Oh, yeah. They were in that too-damn-big needle, and that thing wasn't going anywhere near her person.

She put a hand over her face and sobbed. She felt miserable. Her mother had lied; this was *not* a glorious event in her life. It hurt like a motherfucker and she didn't want to ever go through it again.

"Oh, none of that, Rosita, chica, none of that."

She snatched her hand away from her face in shock, and in pain, as another pulse ripped through her. She got a small bit of satisfaction when, upon her vision clearing, she saw a light-brown face screwed up in agony before her.

"*Rosa!*"

She looked down at what she gripped in her hand, realizing it was, in fact, her husband's hand and not the guardrail that had been her friend these past umpteen hours.

"Where the *fuck* have you been!"

Tears leaked out of his eyes, especially since she didn't let go of his hand. "*Rosa!*"

"Ulrich!" she cried, uncaring and unsympathetic of his pain. It was the least he could feel after what she'd been going through thus far.

"I'm not at liberty to say."

"That gotdamn beeper better be off too!" she warned.

Though cognizant of his agony and hers, Ulrich managed to steal a kiss from his wife's stormy lips. "Not allowed to bring them in here. Tim has it in the lobby."

"You kicked Bevin out?"

"No, she went to say hello to her husband. He's been gone as long as I have, chica."

Yes, over two long-ass months. Because she was now living in Ulrich's flat in Virginia Beach, her mother had come up from Orangeburg to make sure Rosita had everything in order. And because she didn't live far from Bevin, the other woman had been checking in almost daily just in case Rosita needed anything, and because it was finally nice to have someone up there who understood what she went through at the drop of a hat. Granted, Bevin got along with the rest of the significant others of her husband's SEAL Team, but she and Rosita had history going back to the single-digit years.

Rosita wanted to say something else, but there was suddenly a draft between her legs and fingers that didn't belong to her or Ulrich prodding around.

"You're ready to go, Rosita!" the obstetrician declared.

Ulrich grinned and kissed her forehead. "Seems my baby waited for her daddy after all."

Rosita just huffed. *Bastard.*

Bevin returned just in time for the first push. With her two best friends holding each hand, Rosita egged on her body to expel the child that had been conceived the spring prior. It was excruciating and lasting much too long for her liking, and then...it was over.

"Ah, damn," Ulrich breathed. "That's a baby!"

Rosita would've laughed had she had breath in her body to spare; but instead, she sagged into the pillows at her back and closed her eyes, Ulrich moving away from her while Bevin kissed her forehead.

"I'm so damn proud of you!" Bevin whispered shakily in her ear.

Rosita kept her eyes closed. "Are you crying?"

"No..."

Liar.

Rosita held Bevin's hand in both of hers and took a few deep breaths, a smile breaking along her face when she heard her child cry for the first time.

"Everything looks good, Mrs. Brown," the doctor said. "A beautiful baby girl you got here."

"Told you!" Ulrich cheered and Rosita shook her head.

"Like he knew his sperm had an X chromosome in it when he knocked me up," she muttered, wincing a little as the nurses helped her deliver the afterbirth.

"I have an intimate connection with my swimmers," Ulrich insisted, his voice sounding closer than before.

Rosita scrunched up her face. "You are so nasty!"

"You married me anyway," he reminded her.

"I was under duress."

"*Mmm-hmm*," Ulrich grunted. "Open your eyes and look at the beauty we created."

Rosita did. Her heart squeezed at the sight of Ulrich holding his tiny daughter in his big, strong arms. The baby looked at him in wonder, and Rosita definitely concurred.

"She looks just like you, I think," Ulrich announced in awe.

"Your mother will be pleased," Bevin teased.

Ulrich smiled. "I know I am. I don't think I'd be a very good-looking woman." He gave his pinky to their child and the baby slapped at it, making him laugh. "Oh, yes, this is definitely your daughter!"

She scowled at her husband. "Hater."

"Nope. I'm more in love than I ever thought possible," he said, tearing his eyes away from the treasure in his arms to look at her. "Te amo mucho, esposa. Gracias por mi hermosa hija."

He placed the baby on her chest. Black eyes looked up at her curiously, and Rosita touched a trembling hand to the head of curly black hair. The baby was closer to her shade than Ulrich's, but she would probably end up darker than both her parents once she got older. Nevertheless, Rosita bent forward and kissed her daughter's crown. "Hi, Sancha."

"Sancha?" Ulrich asked.

"Yes, I think she looks like Sancha," Rosita murmured, looking between her best friend and her husband. "Sancha Neo Brown."

"Um, that's kind of kickass," Ulrich noted. "What does it mean?"

She and Bevin had discussed it at length as they poured over baby-name books, and this name felt right to Rosita's soul. Looking at Bevin again and seeing her nod, Rosita answered her husband's question. "Holy Gift. Sancha is Spanish and Neo is from Botswana."

"Your motherlands," Ulrich said.

"Ours," Rosita corrected. "I may be Cuban, but my ancestors are African, just like yours."

"Well, the majority of them," Ulrich teased, kissing her forehead. "I love the name."

"I'm relieved," she said sincerely.

"Girl, after all the work you put in, the least you could do was name her." He kissed his daughter's temple. "Sancha Neo, welcome to the world, baby."

Sancha punched his nose, and her parents chuckled.

"Let me go tell the others Sancha Neo has made her debut," Bevin said, grazing the baby's cheek with her thumb before leaving for the waiting room. Ulrich went to his haunches so he'd be eye level with his wife and daughter. His large hand settled on his baby's back and Rosita was amazed that such tenderness could come from such strength. There was a bandage along the back of it along with some nicks on a few of his fingers.

"Are you hurt anywhere else?" Rosita asked him.

He looked at her and shrugged. "My abdomen, but you should see the other guys."

Rosita took a deep breath and the baby squirmed on her chest. Ulrich rubbed Sancha's back to calm her.

"Tim's arm is in a sling," Ulrich said. "But he'll be all right."

Rosita was sure Bevin threw an epic fit over that internally; her friend had an amazing ability to put her own feelings to the side, especially if an event wasn't about her. Rosita would talk to Bevin about it as soon as she got a free moment.

Sancha pitched her face forward as if inhaling her mother's scent. Chuckling, Ulrich picked up his daughter and curled her next to his heart. As before, the baby rubbed her face into her father's chest, smothering in his smell and love.

Soon a parade of guests marched in and out of the room. Rosita greeted them all as warmly as her exhausted body would allow. Ulrich didn't relinquish his child, not even under threat of his mother and hers taking him over their knee.

"Ladies, I love you; but after what I just left, I need to hold this blessing close to my heart for a little while longer."

And with that, he promptly melted everyone else's, especially Rosita's.

She held Tim's free hand when he approached the bed and squeezed hard. He grinned lopsidedly and nodded when she eyed his injury.

"Just a dislocated shoulder," he told her, shrugging his uninjured one. "I'll be good as new in no time."

"You better be. You know how crazy Bevin gets whenever you come home with a booboo."

Tim looked behind him, taking a gander at his wife and Ulrich cooing over his goddaughter. "We are some lucky bastards, Ulrich and I." He returned his focus to her and rubbed the back of Rosita's hand with his thumb, mindful of the IV protruding from it. "Thanks for loving him, Rosita."

"Thank you for loving my girl," she returned.

He smiled softly. "That honor is all mine, and I will never take it for granted."

"I know you won't," Rosita said. "So I just ask the next time you come back, you try to do so with fewer and less intensive injuries than this time."

He laughed and kissed her forehead. "Sí, yo haré mi mejor."

The visitation only lasted an hour, everyone vowing to come first thing the next morning. Rosita was able to steal a moment for herself as Ulrich walked Sancha down to the nursery upon the doctor's orders. The baby would be back in another thirty minutes for a feeding.

Rosita placed her hands over her face and whispered a prayer a Dios, a prayer for strength, wisdom, patience, humility, and graciousness. She would be the best mother she possibly could for her daughter, and she would be the best wife she possibly could for her husband.

She didn't jump when she felt hands cover hers, just tilted her face upwards when those hands pulled hers away so lips could kiss hers.

"We got this," Ulrich declared, holding her hands to his heart. "We got this on lock."

"Damn straight we do," Rosita agreed, squeezing his hands.

He smiled and sat right next to the bed, leaning his head against her shoulder and letting his exhaustion overtake him.

Her poor baby.

Kissing Ulrich's temple briefly, Rosita followed him into dreamland with a smile on her face, knowing that instead of being seriously fucked, she was definitely, indomitably, seriously loved.

Related Books

Trolling Nights

Navy SEAL Timothy Capshaw is only in Charleston, South Carolina, for the summer. He's not looking for a romance or even a hookup, but when he sees Bevin on his first night out on the town, he knows she's the one for him.

Coffeehouse owner Bevin Moore is the friend who ensures everyone makes safe decisions when they go out on their Trolling Nights, the nights where her friends look for a weekend fling. Then she meets Tim, and she's certain he's the most dangerous choice of all—especially for her heart.

How will Tim convince Bevin he's the man she hasn't known she's been looking for and that the need for her Trolling Nights is over?

Escort to Tenderness

Small-town intake nurse Ira Jackson has played it safe all her life. She's stayed home with a stable job while her sister and cousin live jet-setting lives. Yet as she approaches the other side of thirty, Ira wants her own adventure.

Big-city CEO Max Worthington is perfectly happy to set Ira up on a free date with someone from his male escort service. She's the cousin of a friend, and it's her birthday. No big deal. Then he meets her. Now the only "someone" he wants her with is him.

One weekend. That's all they're supposed to have. But how can they walk away from the tenderness they've both been searching for all their lives once it ends?

TROLLING NIGHTS Excerpt

They strolled quietly down King Street, looking at all the high-end shops that were closed for the night. Tim's fingers, tangled with hers, hooked into the pocket of his jeans, keeping her close even though she could've put space between them. She liked the heat of him merging within her; and this time, he matched his stride to hers.

They reached the Battery and walked along the water's edge. The waxing moon hung in the sky, and the lights of the harbor twinkled like stars. Bevin leaned against the railing, and Tim set their bag of leftovers down and stood next to her, his back to the railing and staring at her.

"How old are you, Bevin?" Tim asked after a few moments.

She gripped the railing and stood on a bottom rung, looking into the dark water. "Twenty-seven."

"Really?"

"You seem surprised." Bevin chuckled. "Given what I just told you, why wouldn't you be?"

"You looked younger than twenty-seven...not even twenty-five yet."

"Older than eighteen at least?"

Tim chuckled. "We wouldn't be here if I didn't think you were over the age of majority—and by majority, I mean twenty-one."

"That's good to know," Bevin murmured, still looking at the water.

Tim scooted closer to her, his forearm touching hers as he leaned back against the railing. "So..."

"So...how old are you?" Bevin asked, heading off whatever question burned his tongue.

"Thirty."

"Birthday?"

He smiled. "November twelfth. Gonna get me a present?"

"Scorpio," Bevin said with a shiver. "I knew you would be trouble."

"Oh? Why's that?"

Bevin shook her head, refusing to reveal that she, as a Gemini, was insanely attracted to Scorpios sexually, but that the twain weren't the best match relationship-wise.

"Not gonna answer?"

"The Fifth has been pled."

Smiling, he conceded. "Okay, well, can I ask you something else?"

Bevin shrugged.

Tim bent his mouth to her ear, his lips drifting along its sensitive skin. "Why has it taken twenty-seven years for you to find someone worthy of your kisses?"

For more on *Trolling Nights*, visit https://www.sjfbooks.com/crafting/tn.

Acknowledgments

Thank you to all of my readers, mentors, friends, and family for supporting me and my endeavors. Special thanks to Jayha Leigh for encouraging me to write this continuation of *Trolling Nights,* Barbie Pomales for giving it another look over, and, as always, my Patreon supporters.

About the Author

Savannah J. Frierson is a *USATODAY* best-selling and award-winning author penning diverse romance and mainstream fiction full of genuine characters, authentic stories, and passionate feeling.

Find Savannah online at https://www.sjfbooks.com/online.

I'll Be Your Somebody

ISBN-13: 978-1-945568-26-8 (eBook)

ISBN-13: 978-1-945568-27-5 (Paperback)

Published by SJF Books LLC. Printed in the United States of America.

www.sjfbooks.com

Made in the USA
Columbia, SC
11 August 2023